THE PROSECUTOR

Into His Eyes

A bold satire on religious spell-bound clime

Chinenyike Lawrence Ezemagu

Only those who have had the hard experience of once being high to the top and later assuming the status of the lowliest would understand the shoe Stabo found himself putting on. But many have disagreed that it was nonetheless an exoneration for living for the devil. A friend dissuaded him strongly on taking that path, *you could possibly make the devil to live rather for you.* If only Stabo had looked through such a possibility than allowing satan to contract him so cheaply.

Author's Note

In this book, Appiah's ordeals were forgotten when he found a new habitation. But just when he thought he had escaped, the real travail began in earnest. But the expert said that all the calamities would have been avoided if the judgment had come from looking into the eyes of Appiah, not into the scripture. From learning to see fellow humans, not just seeing documents.

THE PROSECUTOR is asking two key questions. In a religiously obsessed and hexed clime, it is asking who you and I see in our living– visions of saints and the angels or visions of your own brothers and sisters living with you in the same environment? Or put more correctly, we so see visions of the heavens that we cannot or are blinded to see through our own very brothers and sisters in our very amidst.

At a very critical time in the prose, the king of Monotoso and his honourable cabinet searched and looked through the pages of the Holy Scripture to make the ultimate decision without first seeing through the eyes of Appiah, the innocent lamb. There their biggest error lied and calamity followed suit. But they did not know it until the attention of the preacher was drawn. There is a biblical version to this – Christ said if you cannot love your brothers and sisters whom you see, how much more God whom you do not see? This can be paraphrased as saying if we cannot see our brothers and sisters living with us, how can we claim to see the heavens? That is the first key question my book is asking every reader. The same Christian scripture related well an account of a Levite (clergy) who abandoned his religious and ministerial rite and prayer to attend to a neighbour before him. This is a typical instance of a true child of God who truly saw God by seeing first his fellow human beings, his neighbors. The deadly crisis in our days is that we want or aspire to live in heaven when we have not lived well on earth.

Between the visitor, Stabo, and the preacher in the book, the latter did not admire the former's early impression of seeing visions of the heavens when he could not see his own very brothers and sisters. To the controversial preacher, 'of what good it is putting a man in the moon when he cannot simply survive on earth?'

At a second degree and more critical dimension, the book preaches indigenous knowledge, indigenous lifestyle, originality. It exposes the knowledge, capacity and courage for a people to be their own true selves. Here the vision of the heavens (or angels and saints) that could hinder people from viewing and encountering their own true selves may be the vision and presence of many aliens – alien names, alien identities, alien cultures, alien policies, alien religion, alien god, alien books, alien beliefs, alien institutions, alien language, alien food, alien fashion, alien music, alien people and many other aliens. This is the time to give back all the aliens, give them away to their origins and sources.

This is a wake-up call and knowledge to turn and look inward and see the vision of the black people own selves. Africa can competently and favourably use her human resources, capacity, gifts, talents, blessings, climate, geography, culture and all endowments to grow her economy, her faith, her finance, her science, her governance, her fashion, her literature, her learning and education. Africa can use her own capabilities to grow her industries and institutions. Africa can use her own capabilities to grow her people and her nation without necessarily relying and depending on the vision of others far away. This is the apt time to look straight and directly into African own eyes, to see into the black race own eyes, to see into the eyes of our own brothers and sisters around us.

Chinenyike Lawrence Ezemagu

1

I saw them

I saw them

What I saw, I see

What is seen is seen

I saw them

He was seen only muffing those words painstakingly all throughout the journey. He was cautioned again and again most times in company of flagellations and scourges but he would cower and succumb to nothing, to no pains, to no tortures and to no authorities. He warded off all inducements and persuasions to talk.

What is it that you saw my son? Tell us, speak boldly.

One of the elders urged and persuaded him to speak while pretending before the people. But the man uttered no words still. He said nothing he had seen but continued in his wittering. Another mocked him saying, *He did not see a thing. What a hell could he see with his earthly eye that sees only earthly beings? Do not be deceived. He has no vision real men have; real men see the heaven. Do not take him serious; listen not to him.*

After some considerable distance and a continual instigation for him to speak, he could only say, *what I have seen and said is the same and one, it has not changed; I said it to you all but you refused to take it and it will stand against you on the day of judgement.*

At this point, drawing nearer to the destination point, one of the men shut him up, *he is mad, the heaven has inflicted him with madness because of what he did, for his blasphemy and profanation; you are surely going to pay costly for this, you shall die less than a dog.* But Appiah continued to keep quiet.

2

The city or rather the group of a religious movement resident in the city has stayed long in the tradition of witch hunt of many accused teachers and members of the brethren labelled and designated as enemies, haters, evil and corrupt brethren whereas in reality and truth they were the weak, the vulnerable and the innocents of the society but lacked the immunities and securities of the big guys who perpetuated atrocious and monstrous acts again and again. The infamous religious community has in her internal laws and governance, the reserved right and capacity to punish members by excommunication, ostracization or even killing usually through the process of drowning in the same water they carried out the baptism of their members by immersion. And they would make silly pronouncement reciting and repeating, *let the same water that once redeemed you in baptism, now condemn you, let it now purify and sanctify your soul by giving up your body, pay for your sins man for wages of sin is death and the soul that sinneth shall die.*

People sometimes entertained and amused themselves talking about such brutal, disgusting and outrageous measures of a laughable religion even in a world that should have been emancipated from Dark Age. In some complicated cases, the voice or judgement of the Preacher on the other end of the city was most sought and respected before taking actions on their victims to gain approval and legitimacy.

Akapa, the name of the city, used to be a haven and one of the most serene parts of the world to live until the crop up of the so-called group of religious sect known for Assembly of Fire and Brim Storm. This was why when the missionaries and their European brothers invaded Africa chiefly with their Evangelization and civilizing mission, capitalism and imperialism; they found the place the most suitable and conducive for their long residence in the riches and resources of Africans.

All members and champions of the Community of Fire and Brim Storm professed one creed. They declared so freely and vehemently that they have come to root out and supplant all sins, corruptions and evils for righteousness to reign and people were greatly following them unreservedly. But they were in the true sense the chief incubators of all corruptions and evils. They laid strong claim that they were committed to the mission of sanitization and purification but it was a disguise, propaganda and a weapon specially designed and established to oppress and suppress the weak, the vulnerable and the innocents of the society who were not gathering with them in their vineyard. A part of the sanitization was what was going on with a man called in a day broad light on Friday morning Appiah.

They sprout up in the latter days of modern civilization (but they were not civilized either in thoughts or practices) in order to preach and uphold the truer and more original faith, chiefly through retreat philosophy – hard and sharp retreat to life and numerous religious traditions with its attendant ridiculous practices manifest and common in flogging members, weird intakes and dress code, senseless doctrines and tenets among others.

The attention of the Church especially Catholic church has been drawn to this unscrupulous development and she was at the bid of fighting and stopping them and bringing their misleading doctrines and activities to a conclusive end, but it was rather decided to allow the injunction of the scripture to prevail: 'if what they do is not of God, they will die out and fade away soon and naturally; but if it is of God, you may find yourself opposing, attacking and fighting God'.

But did they die away?

3

They arrived the place of atonement in the early hour of

Friday's morning. Appiah was seen beside the beach suspended in a pulley to be used to drown him to death in their traditional way. Some mocked and derided him. Others spit on him. Yet, another group of people in alarming indifference passed by like nothing was happening. But many people stood watching. It was from among these onlookers watching the horrible treatment meted out to Appiah and the worst that awaited him soonest that a long, silent and private discussion between two interlocutors emanated.

'Does a church of God treat people this cruel way? The holy church of God for that matter!'

'My dear sister, don't be deceived. This one is not holy. In fact, it is no church of God as far as the true God is concerned. There is indeed nothing holy or good about it; there is nothing Godly to be spoken of it. But people won't hear. They won't readily read the handwriting. Did we not hear of late about a church where the pastor ordered her congregations to feed on grasses like goats all in the name of anointing, miracle or so? And there are many other terrible and unthinkable stuff like that taking place. But our people are so gullible and incurably religious that they are readily available to any nonsense provided that it wears the affidavit of religion; it is connected to God'

'Hmmmm… nawaooo. But come to think about it, they say they are – they say they are church. Yet they carry out such amount of brutality and cruelty on their fellow human peoples of the same image of God'.

'That is true. But it is what they say. Anyone or any people could say anything of themselves. But what matters is whether it is true or not'.

'No religion (of God) has ever in time attempted this…so horrific, so disdainful, too inhuman'

'I disagree with you on this note. It is no more a news item in the history of religion.'

'I don't think I understand you. How do you mean please?'

'Sorry, I am not the one you will get to hear about it. But your big problem is that you don't like reading or making research. Reading makes people to find things out, to know better and ultimately to be able to unlearn and rethink many things they could have known'

'Abeg, save me all this your big big grammar, you don come again. All this talks na because I ask you to explain what you mean. Abeg tell me sharp sharp, I promise to give you my food at home or better still, take you out this weekend to shoprite, oya talk ….. hear about what?'

The second woman lowered her head slightly down this time to think through something. Something that had always given her serious trouble as well as any other concerned and meaning citizens. It was the mention of shoprite. It was not the case that she detested the foreign business establishment which has speedily taken over the entire nation. It was rather how the company like other foreign businesses too had taken over the economy of the country without commiserating local establishments. As if that was not enough, the same country that has the company has maintained long hostility to the citizens of the country that has warmly and widely accepted her. Her beloved country and fellow citizens were suffering from xenophobia again and again as well as numerous extraditions from other countries. But she did not blame any of the countries as she continually did with her country whose leaders have consistently refused to build and develop their own country and grow better viable economy. She was extremely concerned with the fact that the foreign agencies were taking all the businesses and economy of her country which could not reciprocate the same and has failed woefully and consistently to create wealth, productions, exports and foreign investments. Rather foreign loans had increased over time unabatedly. Yet, she did not allow the lone thought to take her attention too far from the conversation.

'So, you want to deny that you have not heard about religious tortures and wars - Muslim jihad or holy wars or Christian Crusades or even the highly dreaded Spanish Inquisition or witch hunts or anti-Semitism or the Lord Resistance Army of Uganda and their attendant banes and miseries brought upon humanity. They all, though no more in our present time as carried out then, belong to religion. The inquisition tortured people more than what we are seeing at this place'

'Hmmm ... what we are seeing here this morning is certainly not new. The saying 'there is nothing new under the sun is not untrue'

The second person agreed while she continued to listen in disbelief. She froze. She went white. All parts of her almost shut down. Cold goose came over her. Her blood drained and she felt a great nausea all over her. She expressed an unknown doubt,

'Teacher don't teach me nonsense, let it not be that you are fabricating stuff giving me to swallow hook, line and sinker'

'Africans and short memory. Go back to history. That is the key to so many doors and problems'

'History or fiction. Your own very fabrications'

'I don't blame you. I blame myself who chose to talk. Who killed the great Galileo Galilee? Who silenced many other tremendous personal agencies or their enviable profiles and intimidating potentialities aborted and wasted in like fate?'

'The church didn't kill Galileo please, cross check your information; do your homework well'

'Ok, it is clear to me that your problem is bigger than it seems: it is called indoctrination, you have been hexed, your mind has been held spell-bound through brainwashing and you can't ask question or know beyond what you already know. So, educate me sister, who killed him, and why did the church have to come out openly to render apology after many decades of years?'

'What you don't seem to understand is that there are different accounts pertaining to this incidence. And one has to be careful of which one he or she submits gullibly to.'

'Just tell your own account or version and stop this dangling and dancing around without proofs'

'Well, what I know for certain according history is that the church refuted and pushed back errors, doctrinal errors and all those she persecuted and sanctioned were outlaws, heretics and apostates and more of any of the like-description. Period! You can go on to say trash or whatsoever you feel like... you are entitled to your own opinion .... but don't forget the church is still alive...

'...still alive, right?, lurking around abi? I pray they don't catch me. Or my story will be worse than Galileo. What will I say to my mama and papa, say, I am expending energy and risking my freedom on what I don't even know about?' The duo laughed and laughed again for the very first time since coming in contact with the horrible morning scene that had generated their debate.

'Thank God you know very well that you don't even know... and here you want to come and kill yourself for nothing, ontop matter wey dem never even dream to born your papa and mama when it happened....' They laughed again and even more loosely and resumed their chats.

'Now answer the following questions'

'Yes, Professor'

'Have you heard of water torture?'

'No'

'It was one of the most brutal methods adopted by the inquisition in torturing the so-called reprobates. It was used to torture the condemned sinners; their stomachs were filled forcefully with water through their mouth with the nostrils closed'

'Jesús Christ'

'Have you heard of heretic fork?'

'No'

'What about the hanging cage,

'No'

'Judas cradle',

'No'

'Stack'

'No'

'Scold bridle',

'No'

'Pear',

'No'

'Breast ripper etc'

'No, I have not; I have no knowledge of all those. Could simply explain, oga Professor?'

'They were all instrument of torture and death as well. The pear was particularly used for the women in their vagina to tear through; the breast ripper as the name suggests was used on the women's breast to pierce and rip out their breasts to give them hard agony before dying'.

'please oga professor stop, this is too much, too horror'

'O yeah, too horror just to hear but they actually happened, people experienced them more than what we are seeing this morning …… well, I blame some of these disgusting and appalling incidences to the unknown influences of literatures and certain teachings that could be wrongly adopted and domesticated. Nothing can wield enormous influence in the society like books and the media. Any wonder, they are part of the strong agents of socialization'

'How again do you mean exactly. You are never done with issues and raising dusts. Anyway go on, forge ahead, shake the table, let me see where am gonna fall this time. What do you mean please?'

'You remember the popular passage where it is strongly admonished that anyone who receives a prophet because he is a prophet will receive a prophet's reward; anyone who gives a prophet a cup or glass of water because he is a prophet will receive a prophet's reward?'

'Yes, I do vividly recall. But I don't seem to have any issues about it. Or do you?'

'Neither do I. I have no quarrel with receiving or giving a drink to a prophet or man of God. My quarrel is in doing so just because it is a prophet. The reason given is not profound enough. It is too simplistic and shallow.'

'So, it has resulted unbeknown to number of cases in our world particularly a religious obsessed and hexed clime like ours where people take rubbish or anything just because or for the sake that it is a prophet, he or she is called man of God'

'Oh, I see you have started doing great listening. That is impressive thinking there. You are right on point. Your understanding has improved. Your thought is profound. Like you rightly explained, such book or rather passage of the holy book, is not surprising and impossible, has over time and across different situations initiated, generated, instigated and caused unhealthy interpretation and understanding to gullibly do things and indulge graciously in awful, terrible and condescending lifestyles not for more profound cause but just because it is a pastor; it is a reverend, it is the church, it is written so and so on and forth'

'I think people should do things for more profound reason and not just because a pastor said so. A reverend said so. The church said so. Bring this and that … this or that money. Do this and that. Do not do so so so so..'

They stopped awhile and gave their attention for sometime to the scene of Appiah's torture with water about to be drowned. They hissed. They groaned almost in pain. They protested inwardly. But they stood helpless. They boiled within. They were helpless to the entire situation. They could only pray and hope that some miracles occur. It made one of them to see much of the blame in their conversation to come rather from the people than the teacher and writer of the passage they discussed.

'The blame is actually, I think, more on the people because the teacher clearly stated doing or carrying out such act 'because it is ... ' which implies that it is either it is a prophet or not. The two cannot be possible at the same given time. Therefore, those who abuse the people are not really prophets or men of God. In other way, the teaching first charges us to know who is a prophet before receiving or doing anything'.

'Yes, I agree with you. You have a point there. But what you are planning to go into is not as simple as you have presented it. It involves the big question of knowing. The experts call it epistemology or the nature of knowledge. How do you know, how much can you know; how do you even know what you know? The most genuine ones of all times among them have also manipulated and used their followers. It is why I preferred and proffered reason should be ultimate guide and authority'

'It is contained in that old saying, 'the more you look, the less you see?'

'Oh yeah, that is it. Again, and most importantly, *every evil cries one message – I am good*

'Yes, you are right. God will help us. We will get there one day.'

'Oh yea, we will get there. We have always been saying it. That appears more of consolation theology or rather more correctly, continually living in make-believe world – wishing, wishing and wishing – another dangerous mark of our society and poor quality of our people.'

'The passage has also a sister.'

'Sure? It seems the table has finally turned around. The student has ultimately emerged the professor. Congratulations ma! Oya, talk, your servant is listening.'

'It is a simple one. It is a popular one too. 'Touch not my anointed and do my prophet no harm''

The two laughed again and again and in a very mischievous outlook just as naughty as they were.

'Well, at long last, what is key and must not be ignored easily is that the misinterpretation, adoption and appropriation of such texts letter by letter can and has been very misleading and horrible; books are very powerful, serious caution should be put in place when giving teachings. The teacher might not be there to explain all s/her intended or meant and audience are left to survive on their own, getting only what each makes of it'

4

The onlookers were driven by some members of the congregation. They scattered and went their different ways. Yet people kept passing but not allowed to stand watching the scene. But some mob would build up still after a passing moment. A little girl ran towards Appiah to console him but she was stopped, scolded and driven away. After a while, a mad man appeared from nowhere to laugh at the group of the persecutors.

The madman distracted the morning assembly. They were initially amused at him, his bizarre look and intrepid utterances. He yelled at them, he recounted all their secret sins and dangerous habits: he called them adulterous, murderers, traitors, criminals etc. It was so dramatic. A rare moment the hunters were hunted. The madman indicted them of having always hunted and persecuted the innocents whose bold lives were threats to them; in the same way and manners that their forebears hunted and persecuted the virtuous so they too do and they would perish if they did not turn away from their evils. He challenged them firmly. He faulted them severely. People attempted to ignore him because he was insane, but as they tried to do it, they also came to consider the message irrespective of the messenger.

There was a grave silence. Everywhere was calm; everyone was still and watching in awe. The current of the water flow intensified; cool air blew all over the place. The sun became more visible; every shadow of the night disappeared and paved way for the brightening and brighter morning. Listening to all the utterances of the mad man, their heart broke, their spirit failed and they recoiled quickly to their selves. They knew that they have not been fail to Appiah. They knew that they have hunted and persecuted him unjustly. They searched for way to kill him still but without provoking the rage of the people, without going to suffer the accusation and wrath of the public.

They congregated among themselves. They whispered. They purred. And they deliberated privately. Secret consultation was on for a passing moment. One of them who was the chief persecutor came forward with a suggestion among them.

Seeing the man, the people always recalled the terrible and manipulative measures through which he meandered and manoeuvred his way to the position of the chief persecutor. Many said that he long foresaw or anticipated a day like today and it was fundamentally why he lobbied and wanted to the elevated position of the chief prosecutor. He had always wanted to weaponize the position and power against his enemies or those who did not agree with him in his evil ways. He had always wanted to fight Appiah with that position.

The chief prosecutor was called Stabo. Story has it that he lobbied for the enviable position and through his uncle who was the overseer of the church or congregation, his victory and success were not challenged by anyone no matter how competent. He, it was that proposed that suffering should be imposed on Appiah with an offer of escape. They agreed unanimously to put Appiah in a tight corner, to make an (evil) offer to him. They went to him in private to ask him to make a fake confession of evils he was accused of, and clemency would be granted to him; the church (as the congregation continually called itself) would say to the people that the sinner had been pardoned if he had yielded; for the power to forgive sins reside in the church the body of Christ who is merciful just as the heavenly Father.

You know our son that it is not sensible that we bring this multitude this far and just leave the scene without giving to them what we have prepared them for. But you look at it this way: if you can feign a confession, we will explain to them that the sinner has finally repented and there is no more need for his death and destruction.

But they did not mean their promise; they were no honest with their words. It was pure manipulation. They rather wanted so that the people hear the accused confess and accept the charges brought against him and they would stand upon that to justify their action. So, they charged him to recant and repent.

But Appiah who was blessed with discernment understood all their gimmicks and hoax. Understanding the stunts of his persecutors, Appiah did not do as requested. He made no public confession. Seeing that they were making no impressions notwithstanding all the pressures mounted heavily on him, they resumed their private talks and conspiracy. This time it was so hard for them to come up with another ploy to condemn and put him to death without offending the public. The crowd was already complaining asking for his release especially after the necessary distraction from the mad man. The cool air at the water side blew hard and harder. The morning sun had started to show itself more proudly and elegantly.

Finally, they came to think of something. Somebody. He was the preacher who lived by the city margin. He was a man that the generality of the people had trust in. The persecutors resorted to achieve their aim through him. They planned to ask him to pass death verdict on Appiah and he would secure his own favor.

There had been times the preacher approached the church to make amend for the past times of variances particularly over land disputes and territorial rivalry. The preacher extended hand of fellowship but he was not welcomed. He was continually turned down. Or rather, the conditions given to him were too high. The preacher and the church had long been at loggerheads, fighting secret wars. The rivalry of the two parties had become a very popular one. One that would take certainly yanky years and costly sacrifice to redeem and restore. That sacrifice was Appiah. So they judged.

They calculated that it would be a propitious time to grant to the preacher what he had always wanted using Appiah as a bait. And if the preacher failed to cooperate and play along, they will blackmail him, cut ties with him, ruin his ministry and drive him out of the city joining alliance with the university authority who had always judged the preacher and his activities as enormous nuisance around the town and they have been so anxious to see him no more.

But what they did not know was more than they assumed to know.

5

The preacher was standing with the crowd in one of the streets leading to the university gate. He was attending to different people, giving teachings and counsels at sometimes and praying at another time. Today a university don came to reprove and remove him from this spot, and to stop him from coming and preaching and defying the academic environs, a grand citadel of proficient learning and monumental excellency.

The professor's field of expertise was philosophy. He was one of the professors and scholars whom students and almost everyone have the impression of atheist but the professor would want to disagree and argued quite forcefully that not going to church or belonging to a religious body or sect does not necessarily make one an atheist or means that he did not believe in God. He said that everyone has God and God is for everyone not an exclusive possession of some acclaimed few; but religion was not for everyone or even harsher than that, it was not necessarily relevant, if it was only for the purpose of seeking and finding God who is in every region and everyone he has created.

The professor, therefore, took to what he called regular unceasing communion with his creator and maintained a deep personal, ever growing communication and relationship with Him staying away from organized religion and religious dramatizations. He went further to fault the preacher and all religions as mechanized tools of easily controlling and misleading the masses through indoctrination and brainwashing.

For one thing, the professor scared many away from himself due to this unpopular charisma in a religious spell-bound clime and for a very long time, he was never seen as saved but one of the lost sheep of Israel, a damn sinner of the kingdom of the vain earthly world. Or better still, another earthly eye without heavenly visions of God and the angels, a wasted soul. He was a definition of what many called antichrist.

Notwithstanding the open confrontations of the university institution and rebukes from the professor, the preacher was relentless, determined, dogged and tenacious. He was giving up not. He was fighting faithfully to the end. He too returned allegations to the professor, accusing him of attacking and persecuting God, his children, his church and his minister (s). The most outrageous and weird statement that amused the professor so much and since then he had never taken the preacher serious, was the arrogant, poignant and repugnant claim of being the son of God who has come or been sent again in the modern time to complete the travails of man's redemption and sanctification. But the professor as well as many of his colleagues treated this as the height of religious irrationality and insanity ubiquitous in a deteriorating and imploding society, a big mark of pre-scientific society, Dark Age, total backwardness and attack on reason.

But for the numerous members of the public or the generality of the society, this was not so, the situation was clearly a different thing. So they rather went and rushed after the preacher. They truly saw and treated him as the son of God in the modern time as acclaimed and portrayed by the bearer which some few others judged to be a clear demonstration of religious naivety, vulnerability, gullibility and porosity.

A lot of people went to the preacher more than the Church of Fire and Brim Storm. Or rather, since the emergence of the preacher, he had pulled more weight and members of the society that formerly aligned with the church switched allegiance and alignment to follow him. It was this problem of who got the higher population than the others that has created and resulted to the strongest tension and fraction and rift between the duo. And the preacher most oftentimes was not prudent at all. He was not helping in any efforts to douse the tension and ameliorate the already deteriorated situation. He would rather appeal to the scriptures referring to himself as the 'Christ' and the church as 'John the Baptist' who has arrived the place earlier to prepare his coming and announce him to the world. And the people who were now the disciples or followers of 'John the Baptist' had to abandon John to follow Christ. By the way, has John himself not announced so publicly that he had to decrease while Christ increased. This was one of the numerous and loft claims of the preacher that put him in longer enmity with the popular congregation or church.

The preacher was damn arrogant with words and analogies and it did not help in any way to quell and alleviate the already troubled situation. This has caused fractions too among the people and resulted to a big rift between the church and the lone preacher. For this, the duo has not agreed on many things. And they had been at loggerhead for far too long. Each weighed enormous influence and pulled weight in their own respective jurisdiction, in their own right. But the church hoped that they could agree on the matter of Appiah and possibly find reconciliation and reunion in the expected judgement.

Many who flooded to the preacher came with questions about the laws of God, knowledge about God, about sins, about prayers, about judgment, about heaven and hell, about salvation, about demons and more. Others came with stories and troubles and challenges of life, families, works, marriage, relationship, leadership. And the preacher, it was said had truly offered good answers to their questions and solutions to their problems many times. He offered wonderful and impressive counsels and strategies about life, family, marriage, relationship, leadership and others. Nkadu, the king of Lomonoto kingdom owned his good and astute leadership to the great counsels of the preacher.

One day a family came to see the preacher. It was about family matter and economic backwardness. The family related to the preacher that they were not happy because they all stayed and slept in a single room. The preacher listened indulgently. When they were done with their pathetic story, he was silent for some time. He took a deep breathe, stared at the couple and offered quite a bizarre and crazy solution but in the end it was result proven. He asked them, in a religious and divine tone, to go home and take along with them their livestock into the room and live that way for a week and return or report back. They returned after a week and the preacher asked them this time around to go and remove the livestock and still come back. When they returned, the preacher inquired about their feeling, they expressed excellent and positive feeling. The preacher taught them contentment.

But the same professor would out rightly challenge this and argue insistently that it was called catastrophe philosophy or feeling good or consolation theology. Catastrophe philosophy, the professor had explained, is an easy way of explaining a bad situation with a worse one and the worse with the worst and the worst with the worse worst, and it continues in such circle infinitely without taking responsibility of a problem; without choosing and working towards improvements; it is a convenient way of using worse situations to console, pacify and ultimately escape from facing the real problems squarely for the sake and purpose of creating and enjoying good feelings as against hard and ill feelings.

Other times, the preacher related his teachings in simple stories to impart lesson. He encouraged people to seek God but also to be aware of places of God or places called God's house. Or even harsher than that, he profaned, according to some purists, in saying that churches are not Godlier than any other places outside the church and many acclaimed houses of God can be more bedevilled than the outer world.

This was what partly or essentially explained why the preacher never owned a building called church; he preferred and chose the outer open space and he was indulged in using this as imagery or allegory to explain that God is everywhere, in the open space, in the open air accessible by all and sundry, not enclosed by any structures and authorities. The preacher made those indicting statements during one of the old days of rivalry and conflict with the Fire and Brim Storm Church.

That very day, he had told a curious story of a boy who lost his bicycle by the street side of hoodlums and bagabums but after sometime he recovered it. Then the little boy went into the church with immense joy and gratitude to pray in appreciation to God but when he came out, he never found the bicycle again in his entire life.

His story of two women fish sellers amused so many people but very impressive in many ways. It was one of his usual stories gathered from the guru from the East. Returning from the market, the night caught up with two women fish sellers on their way home and they decided to pass a night by their friend's house which was close by. That night they were well entertained and shown their room for the night. There came a trouble.

In the middle of the night or after some minutes of occupying the room, the guests felt quite unease and deranged. They tried to endure it but it was not working out. Finally, they invited their host friend, explained that they perceived unpleasant odour that could not allow them to sleep. She was amazed and bewildered. She could not possibly think of anything with a bad smell inside the bedroom except the good rosy flowers she had innocently and strategically arranged and placed around the room not only to decorate and beautify it but more essentially for good smell and feeling and to give to her friends a warmth reception and the best treatment she could afford.

The host woman was a wife of a great gardener and she kept so many flowers in the house. She herself could not smell any bad odour from the room except the aura and fragrance of the followers. She finally came to disclose to her guests about the flowers she had used to decorate their room. At that point, the two fish sellers unanimously consented that it was the flowers that was the cause of the bad smell.

What did they do? They took the flowers outside the room and brought in their baskets of fish which had been outside, and for once, they could feel calm, relieved and were able to close their eyes to sleep quietly and peacefully. He quoted the original owner of the story at the end remarking: bad smell, good smell, who can tell it?

The preacher particularly related this story during his encounter with the scholar professor. And he meant to use the story to demonstrate how things or reality appears differently to different people; how people could out rightly reject the good which is God, the good news, salvation, the church and the chosen one which rightly the one, he was. Things appeared and meant different things to different people depending on who they are, their background, environment, influences, knowledge base and more. The preacher remarked conclusively.

Meanwhile, the religious sect of prosecutors did not want to come to the preacher in an open place because they dreaded the public/crowd. So they thought of what to do. Some suggested to keep Appiah in a locked-up room until the preacher was available for them in a more private place most certainly in the later part of the evening when everyone had retired from public engagements to their homes. This they all yielded to in unison and waited to re-convey at the appropriate time to meet with the preacher in an enclosed setting.

Their decision was never a shock to the preacher. The preacher had always known them to be enemies of the open space; they never liked open space. Yet, he never used secret cult, secret society to describe them. His imprudence with words was never to that height. Or maybe, it was rather the case that he did not really know them in toto.

6

About the midday, Appiah entertained a guest in his locked-up apartment. Lo and behold, it was the chief persecutor, the same person who had suggested and championed the death plot at the river side. Appiah was surprised to see him. Or he was not. He knew too well how the chief persecutor had always been on him to recant and repent under duress even where he has nothing to repent about.

The chief persecutor began to announce to him that he has come to talk with him about his sins or rather his boring sincerity that was seriously becoming sins in the city and it would silence him if he did not withdraw from it. He drew closer to him and promised him that they had a closed door and nothing about the visit and their conversation would be known or revealed by anyone or to a third party. He proceeded to threaten him that by the end of the day, the preacher would be passing his verdict on him and that would amount definitely and instantly to his end on this earth. He recoiled backward, and moving ahead closer to Appiah, he leaned again and began,

'What madness moved you to begin to discuss and disclose what you saw underground the building of the sanctuary? In fact, it is an inner underground chamber no one dares to go to and that is if at all it is known to anyone except the privy members'.

Appiah was mute, staring keenly at him. He was filled with all dots of cold all over his body. He was shocked beyond doubt. Or he was not. He had always suspected the chief persecutor was a very notorious fellow. But his wildest imagination did not tell him that he must be a hard-core cultist or the personified demon of the society. Appiah stared helplessly with all the goose registered on his look. He went white. His kneel knocked again and again. His Nicodemus visitor continued,

'I warned you the first day I caught you down there. Your curiosity is overbearing and it has put you into damn shit. Boy, you have succeeded shitting your own very self. Look very well, the shit is all over you. Everything you did that day I found it out. You found the mystery book and read about the account of the sons of our leader and how castrated and impotent a man he is. But that was not all. You are not the only one who know or have knowledge about things. Many people you see walking the street know more than you can imagine. I told you that the most knowledgeable person on the face of the earth works every day cautiously and assiduously to keep to himself what he knows without assuming the condition of a town crier. Time and again, I appealed to you for your own good to keep your mouth shut else it would be shut forever. You failed to abide by the chief principle of any seer which is silence'.

'But I did. I cooperated with you. It was only when the greater part of the evils done right under the sanctuary of God persisted that I could no longer hold it; someone needed to speak out. I am the only one who could speak; I am the only person who has seen it'.

'We are saying practically the same thing. It happened that way because you did not heed to my caution; you were able to see more perhaps beyond what you could keep because you persisted in going there and reading up more. I asked you to do only your duty at the temple as the chief temple watch without meddling into matters or places that you are not meant to. It is simply called boundary'.

'So you are defending that you should be having sex with your own daughter just for your cultic ritual…. and other disturbing things I had come to find out and I could no longer keep just like the sex culture with your daughter, Mithras/black mass, other rituals, horrors …. Just name it?'

Appiah was still speaking and completed his thought with a spit on the floor.

'Shut your stinky mouth there. Speak no more. Whatsoever is done in there is none of your business. Since you choose to discover, how many can you discover, how many have you discovered; even one percent of the things done there and about the sanctuary/church, can you know it? I am talking to you, I am asking you Mr researcher or speaker of the truth, the only true prophet in our Age. Answer me!'

'I see…. So this is why you decided to connive with your daughter to frame me up to be the person raping her instead'.

'You have yet seen anything. What you will see awaits you soonest. The horror of your own death. But there is an escape route for you to consider well boy; if you trust me, if you can work with me'

'And what is that? I am sorry. I can never trust you. You are not a caliber of person I work with. Working with you will ruin my reputation and image'.

'I am asking you for the last time, now that you still have some time left, before the final whistle goes for the end of this phase of your life in this world'.

'You can talk to me but you cannot certainly buy my conscience. You cannot do injury to me or my soul. It is well known that evil man cannot hurt or do harm to another man more virtuous than he is'.

'Appiah, I thought you were smarter than this. But you proved me wrong since the day I did not know what spirit that compelled and led you to see what you saw, and as if that was not yet enough, you could not abide by a simple discipline of silence. You should have learnt that the saying has changed; it is no more punish only the one that commits the crime. Rather it is reversed. So, 1 urge you earnestly, be up to date, be updated, stop living in the past, in your little private imagination, the world is going bigger and more sophisticated. Or you will pay costly'.

After some silence, the chief persecutor resumed the dialogue. He questioned Appiah on a number of matters in strong bid to illicit information, and related finally,

'Even the appointments to the position of the senior pastors in the church in the recent past, the appointees are mostly my own relations and friends. Your name was to be the first but you have not convinced me to do so yet. You need to prove it to me that you will work with me. You need to gather with me not to scatter while am busy gathering. I persecute you because I want as every man would do, to protect my own interest, my own family first – remember self-preservation is key – don't be a dummy, don't be a nerd. But notwithstanding, I still love you, I still have some soft spot for you and it is because of this I am here'.

'So, what do you really want from me?'

'Now you are talking. This is a better way to engage, a more civic way than aggressions and hostilities. This is the clever boy I had always known'.

'Speak please'

'I propose to offer you a second chance which you can never get anywhere in the entire world; I ask you now to follow my instructions and do my bidding in order to escape from this city now to far unknown place and never return again or it will be to your own peril or return only when this generation has passed on'

'What would the people think happened to me?'

About your where-about, don't bother at all, I will personally take care of it; it will be explained to the public that you escaped like many prisoners do'

'Point of correction, I am no prisoner please. Use your language well'

'Well, somewhat you are. You cannot deny that fact. You better face the reality squarely. You have lost your freedom like all prisoners. And a kind man as myself is here to restore it to you'

Stabo the chief prosecutor paused for a moment and continued.

'Or if you don't like that suggestion, maybe because you don't want to be associated with the numerous number that have escaped from our prisons at will, always overpowering the entire powerful armed forces of the nation regardless of all the billions and trillions squandered on security and military gadgets and maintenance time and again'

'Just the same way you have been squandering the resources of the church'

'Let us don't talk about that now. We might be distracted and swayed from the main course. Rather, let us face what is here before'

'And what is that?'

'There is a better option to be considered, this one will certainly please you more: being an innocent or virtuous man, you prayed intensely, the heaven opened and the angels of God came to take you away. Recall vividly that there are many told precedents or I should say legendary, it happened to Paul and Silas while in the prison, to Daniel before the den of lions and even Jesus escaped the tomb; so why can't it happen to you as well and why won't the people believe it too when 1 propagate the story? We have propagated so many bigger or more serious stories, narratives, beliefs and information than this. This is just nothing compared to what many believed to be the truth in this world. This is nothing compared to the myths and lies that have over time ruled our society. And today, they are revered as sacred and infallible, packaged, doctored and canonized. I mean painting the picture so well like a good artist. You are a virtuous man, remember that and never forget it'

'Stop the heresy, enough of the blasphemy. For your information, all the instances you have brought out were never painted. They all happened real'

'Hmmmmm…. Were you there? You Speak with so much certainty and indubitability; learn to report child, not assertions that reveal stack ignorance and dastard dependence. Anyway, it is not good for us to digress and deviate from the main issue. We cannot abandon the breast for any lump-like protruding structure, so tell me your mind…'

The chief persecutor pressed on again and again for another half an hour but to no avail. To his shocking dismay, Appiah turned down his offer; it pained him down to his bone marrow that for a second count he did not accept to take his Greek offer. 'But he is certainly not going to escape it the third time. First time and second time may be experiments, but the third will be a confirmation'. The chief persecutor pulled himself together and gathered momentum and fortitude from those consoling words. Appiah suspected or did not trust the second offer of the chief persecutor just as the first. He suspected he was going to kill him in the disguise of helping him to escape while he (Stabo) would proceed to concoct and paint all the stories he was good at creating and propagating. Appiah rather preferred meeting with the preacher and facing the possible outcome.

The story of Appiah and Stabo the chief persecutor is a perfect account of friendship gone sour. Appiah invaded his secret corner and accessed his top-secret. But the friendship was still on and going until Appiah refused to go his bidding. The condition Stabo gave him for doing what he did was going to join and become one of them. Stabo told him that he could no longer be two persons; he could no longer be here and there. He had to choose to be one of the two. As he had seen what the general public did not know about, it was time he got into the inner caucus fully and participate and do what they did or got cut out completely. Inevitable travail culminating in untimely and unfortunate death was the definition of the total cut.

Stabo promised his prospective recruit all manner of opportunities ranging from wealth, connections, pleasures and powers. His emphasis was on the power to seeing visions or prophecy and controlling the people. But Appiah was again very patronising and repudiated his offer. Appiah told him that he was not in need of any fake visions and boasted that there was a sufficient vision he enjoyed every passing day. That vision was the vision of his own brothers and sisters he lived and worked with in the same roof, compound, neighbourhood, community and country. It was indeed the last meeting between the duo before the outbreak of his torment and tribulation. Right from that moment, it was clear to Appiah that it was not going to be a smooth ride. Yet, he did so little or nothing to help the situation. Or he was just over confident.

7

At sunset, they were all at the premises of the preacher.

Many people have retired from duty. They met grave silence; the preacher was nowhere to be located. They called and called. They knocked at the doors again and again. They searched and combed round all the apartments and the vicinity. What shocked them more was that the doors were left wide open.

It was gathered that the preacher had been kidnapped. His prophecy had finally come to pass. The killers of good men and all prophets of old have finally got prey of him. Some said his kidnappers were from the university he had been terrorizing and profaning with his preaching, religious messages, seductions, threats and mind control of the people like *accept Christ or perish; without Jesus, there is no life.* His grey big gate and most of his doors and walls were registered with this caption and many others in the same genre.

The nearest suspect was the philosopher don but none was certain of this unfounded speculation. Others said that the missing of the preacher had utterly nothing to do with the scholar. The long-stayed quarrels and exchange of words in many ways and manner including the media and the kidnap were only a mere chance. But it was such a bad time for there was no time for anyone to indulge in such critical analysis and distinction. No one had the luxury of time to search for casual relation or no casual relation.

Some others thought probably he was attacked by some other hoodlums and miscreants. Yet, some opined that he had gone to the mountain to offer prayers and sacrifices. This was a part of him most people particularly his followers knew too well about him. But this submission was not considered serious because of the entire disposition of his residence. Practically everywhere were open and unsecured.

Meanwhile, the chief persecutor was lost in his own lone preoccupation. Not the unknown fate of the preacher. Not the possible ordeal everybody was worried about concerning the sudden disappearance of the preacher. No, not at all. But his own selfish end. For him, damn whatsoever ugly fate that could have befallen him. Who cared? For whose sake? But the goose had easily and momentarily forgotten that it was partly for his own sake, his own very wicked and impious end. He sure needed him to also achieve his ulterior motive.

Buried in his own negative thinking, he imagined how he had plotted to bring Appiah before the preacher with the mob causing serious damage to his reputation. He would build all kinds of falsehood and allegations of numerous abominable evils and crimes before the preacher and move to demand for his victim's death. He had put up all efforts to influence the decision of the preacher by bringing to his consciousness what he stood to gain, the reconciliation and reunion he long sought. In his figment of imagination, he had seen the preacher in his unique style to be quiet for a moment, after which he took a deep breathe, gazed at the people one after the other and coughed out a death sentence on Appiah to their wonder and bewilderment. But he needed to wake up from his delusional *chateau*.

A quick tap on the shoulder helped him tremendously to do so. The tap quickly alerted and woke the chief persecutor from his flight of thought. It was one of his men coming to him and demanding to know the next course of action. Meanwhile, everyone in the assembly was already getting tired and fed up with the entire prosecution. Some began to reinterpret it as God being on the side of the victim; it was the invisible finger of God saving Appiah. By the way, the first time, it was the appearance of a strange madman; now it is the disappearance of the preacher. It ought to be discerned and regarded. It was worth more just a coincidence or chance or any reckless unfolding of events. It was also this section of the people that suggested and interpreted that the preacher was not missing. Rather he was abreast with the entire development through a vision or divine ministration and left the house. He did not want to be involved in the dirty deal and decided to go into hiding like Elijah the prophet of old. It was this the same people who pointed to the rest of others to see an inscription the preacher had left at one corner of his wall

'If only I were with no sins and faults, I would have gladly yielded to condemning and approving his death'

They were still for a moment. They did not condemn him again and started parting one after the other. The chief persecutor also the archenemy was furiously in rage and boiling all over. In quick seconds, his eyes came into contact with Appiah and with strong reflex he withdrew his eyes.

Someone and one of the few who had believed and supported Appiah came over from his back and whispered gently,

It will pay you more to withdraw this entire prosecution or I should say aimless hunting of the innocent just as you have withdrew your very eyes moment ago; follow the deep message of your eyes and listened to the profound voice of truth.

The persecutor was even more enraged and restless. Seeing his rage and entire ugly look, the fellow added, 'do you wish to punch me? Wake up from your dream; I am no Appiah. I will expose you and all your evil exploits. I will set you to dance endlessly without music. Learn for once in your damn life not to offend the wrong person. I am no standard of yours. I will make you kiss the floor in perpetuity. Do you wish to see your own ears without a mirror or to maintain your daily intake without passing out all your miserable life? Then, count, with your tongue, your own teeth; be wise and set the innocent free'.

The chief persecutor was an unrepentant demon in the hood of religious affidavit. Everyone knew this too well but he was practically an untouchable deity. Everyone knew this and of course, his challenger that evening, but it was shocking why the fellow still had the guts to put up the open confrontation as though he was damn clueless of his vulture-some life. Even when another person cautioned him to withdrew his statements and beware of a man of God, a bishop and chief persecutor for that matter while quoting the popular scriptural passage, *touch not his anointed and do his prophets no harm*; the fellow was even more unorthodox and eccentric,

'Save me that rubbish. You people are so religious spell-bound and chained that you cannot see or think but take anything clothed and coated as God. Listen carefully to this, this thing you quote 'touch not my anointed and do my prophet no harm', I am certainly no party to it. I am liberated and fully prepared to walk in no one's shadow; many of these drafted and fabricated injunctions, doctrines and stories that perpetually induce and impel you to bury your human reason. The only anointed I recognize is one who lives well, does the right thing and loves his fellow humans. Nkrumah, Mandela, Azikiwe, Senghor, Nyerenye, Prempeh, and many more were anointed. Martin Luther was. Rowlings was highly anointed. Our nationalists and heroes who fought for us and resisted foreign invasions and dominations were exceedingly anointed. And so many others who saved and did not destroy humanity; they saved lives and did not deceive and delude others in order to survive and thrive'.

All those dramas brought and left the chief persecutor in his own lonely thought. Perhaps putting some calculations together in his head on how to deal with the hippie who another madness has taken over and compelled to speak sacrilegiously and profane the anointed and consecrated.

The chief persecutor who grew up to take the name Stabo had suffered a very painful past that he took up the Latin future tense name meaning that he would stand in life no matter what it cost him. He oftentimes remembered with deep hurt and throbbing how he had had wonderful outings with his wealthy and influential father who was then one of the powerful politicians reckoned with in the country. Those outings afforded him enormous exposure to a good number of people of high profiles nationally and internationally, to an exalted and elevated lifestyle. But everything in no short time came to turn sour and became a mirage and taunting nightmare for Stabo. He could only sit or lay in his dark self to recall all this with tears because in the present there was almost nothing to show for it, for a life once lived. For this, he was remembered always for saying, 'good things do not come-by easy; yet good things go away easily'.

His powerful father, for reason that was hard if not impossible to decipher, practically abandoned him since junior high school days that throughout his formative years in the secondary and higher institution, he was practically thrown to chances to survive living from hand to mouth, barely paying his school fees and meeting other bills and responsibilities and needs. He was fully aware that people stand on the shoulder of those who have succeeded in order to succeed too. But he became even more aware of the fright that he could never stand on the shoulder of his own very father. Even the friends he had made and other big names he had encountered during the glorious old days, it got dawn to him too that he could not stand on their very shoulder. They blocked him on social media, deleted or blacklisted his contact numbers and totally cut ties with him just because he was not yet where they were, level has changed or rather, his own biological father who had it all around, had all it takes to provide adequately for his family and children, had not offered him what other fathers had generously offered their own children and wards. Even an enemy was not given the kind of treatment melted out to Stabo by his own very father.

Numerous and different explanations have been alluded to in order to explain such an unthinkable, cold and bitter treatment of a father to his own child since college days. Among all the stories alluded to, was the account of Stabo's father being bewitched not to take care of his family. The same account linked it to polygamy. The father of Stabo married different women and it has contributed quite negatively in destroying his home so fast. This account has helped rather to prove that polygamy or marrying many wives is one of the worst things to happen to a man.

All this made Stabo to realize early in life that if he had to stand in life, he had only his own shoulder to reckon with. But he also realized that there was, practically speaking, every need for an external shoulder. 'No one is an island'. He found that shoulder rather in having a pack with the demons, dining and merrying with the devil himself. And colleagues knew him as the only person who had seen the devil face to face alive. He could do anything to achieve his goals. To enjoy more immunity and security, he joined the religious movement and since his membership, he had been damn ruthless, brutal and cruel but only those who could look deeper could see deeper; he always shielded it with so much masking, dogmas and protocols just as he was busy distracting the people following so called due process in prosecuting his prey.

Only those who have had the hard experience of once being high up there and later assuming the status of the lowliest would understand the shoe Stabo found himself putting on.

But many have disagreed that it was nonetheless an exoneration for living for the devil. A friend dissuaded him strongly on taking that path, *you could possibly make the devil to live rather for you. That is the power in every human person but a lot of people seldom see through this and that is if at all they even attempt looking through their immense possibility in life.* If only Stabo had looked through such a possibility than allowing satan to contract him so cheaply.

Buried in his own deep thinking, Stabo recalled the very first time he had a strong misunderstanding with the preacher and it marked the beginning of his hatred for him and by extension, also contributed to the long-stayed rift between the church and the preacher. During the preacher's early period in the city, the inquisitor (Stabo) paid a diplomatic visit to introduce himself. It was rightly supposed to be the other way round; the preacher was to do this for being the new comer to the city but for the fact that he always had secret and evil agenda, he rather went combing for ways to lure him to his party and buy him over. Unfortunately, the preacher was as stubborn as his visitor. Some said that he was another capo in another cabal and did not want to mistake and mingle categories. Certainly, he was the last person to lick others' ass for the purpose of politics and partisanship. He adamantly refused to be a puppet or rather a pawn in the game of chess.

So the chess game started between the church and the preacher over jurisdiction, power, demography, economy and popularity. Their exchange of pleasantries that day was not even friendly because when the visitor was given to showing some unnecessary impression in talking about prayers and seeing visions of saints and angels, the host was also given to sufficient doze of mischief. He gave a patronising comment, 'with all the crowd of saints and angels you are given to seeing, are you able to see your own very brothers and sisters here on earth?'

He made that strong statement in a light note, though still loaded and pregnant with meaning, but the visitor took it to heart and was able and quick to perceive that there was no entry for him going to massage religiously a person of his sort. Stabo knew that it was going to be a rough ride. From a single step he could tell the rest of the thousands of miles in view. He prepared himself ahead.

But from nowhere, amidst all the chaos and dramas, a group of rioters came to seek vengeance for the disappearance or rather kidnap of the preacher. This was probably the preacher's own cartel coming to distract his archenemy and group and set Appiah free. For the first time, it appeared that one party was leading in the game after many years in the past. The strayed group had set Appiah free, abducted and threatened the lives of many. But Stabo, the bad evil, always had his way. Always prepared and alert. He had one day describing himself, quoted, *even the obstacles in my way, I predict them before those that will bring them will start to think about them. I plan for betrayal, I plan for backstabbing. I also plan for reunion and forgiveness long before they happen. I expect nothing, I expect anything, I expect everything.*

He lied. He overhyped himself. Much of what was happening that day and others that had happened in the past, he did not see through them as asserted, else he would not have stressed himself all day investing both energy and time. Even the reconciliation and reunion scheme he had strategized failed him woefully. The bitter fact was that he predicted nothing. He saw nothing. Or it was the case that he was deceived. The only thing he saw was his own vain delusions and insatiable greed and the only thing he perceived was his blind ambition. But he was always prepared. Perhaps he was right in some of those claims. He escaped the pandemonium in a way no one could humanly explain. Mysteriously.

8

Appiah thanked the God of the preacher so profusely and escaped the city to another kingdom instantly. Some said that it was with the great counsel of the preacher that he escaped. But no one was sure of it. But Appiah knew that the chief persecutor has prevailed so much on him without success and would stop at nothing seeing him dead or wasted ruthlessly particularly now that he was a custodian of many of his top secrets. So, he escaped to a neighbouring town called Monotoso kingdom.

Here at the Monotoso kingdom, Appiah found a home again, a home away from home; he found friends and solace. He lived again, farming and doing works within the king's palace. His movements were restricted and he was always guarded for his safety. God greatly blessed the kingdom through him. As Appiah heard in his dream world shortly after his arrival,

Through you my chosen one I shall bless this kingdom and make it prosperous

It shocked Appiah terribly about what he found in the house of the king ten weeks after his arrival. He was always given to finding and seeing. What has he found or seen this time again – more problems or solutions? The king was a very nice person. His leadership was popular and democratically accepted by the people who took great pleasure and admiration in identifying with him as their king and ruler. The king was highly impeccable, just and credible. He was, to the best opinion of many, the best leader the kingdom could have.

The founding of the kingdom contained a curious account of a son who the entire people of a village unanimously consented to be sacrificed following an aged-long tradition to appease the land and the god annually. But the smart father whom it was his family turn to give away his son, tacitly sent the son away from the village in disguise of sacrificing him to the evil forest. Or some said he was sent to war to be positioned in war front for immediate extermination. Yet, some has said he was sold out to the

Europeans. Be that as it may, the son was to be rid off in any way as a ransom and remission of the land and people in accordance to the long-standing tradition. The son escaped to an unknown land, grew into a man throughout the long years and journey of wandering from one forest to another, one village to another until the present settlement where exactly Monotoso kingdom was founded and grown into large and amazing kingdom.

The sitting king who was one of the succeeding generations' leaders told Appiah all this story within the first week of his arrival to the kingdom. It was that the same evening the two were enjoying wonderful chats together that Appiah finally mustered momentum to engage the king in what he had long observed since his self-exile in the house.

'I have, no doubt, become one of you. I feel like every member of the family. I have no feeling of missing my home. All this is because of the kind of manner and ways you have received me, listened to my story and accepted me like a brother. Thank you again and again for this. I remain ever indebted. I cannot say thank you enough.'

'You are always welcomed. You have already said everything. So, I won't bother to appear repetitive. Just know, this is your home. You are welcomed. You are my brother. We are brothers to each other. But we need see it so we can act and live it. I see you as my brother. You see me as your brother too. This is vision of my brothers on which pillar I have lived to build my reign upon just like my predecessors and forebears.'

'I must say that your thought is powerful. The world will be a better place, the earth will be heaven with your kind of ideology. That is the heaven we achieve living well. It is nowhere high above in the sky or in any far distant measures. As my own holy book also agreed, 'the kingdom is here among you'

'You have spoken wisely. You spoke the truth. Truth is not about age or color or sex or race or region or religion or any affiliations or groups. You are smarter than your age'

'I am flattered my king, my brother'

'You can stay more with the last. God alone is the true king and ruler of the entire universe. Don't forget that so that you may not be intimidated or deluded'

'The level of your moral and intellectual capacity as well as consciousness of God even as a king is quite admirable. And I am prompted and compelled to understand certain things I noticed since my arrival.'

'What is it that you have seen brother? Tell me, Speak boldly brother'

The entry of the king caught the attention of Appiah about something. It rang a hard bell in his skull about a memory that usually sent cold shiver to his entire body. The only difference was the 'brother' identity. It was after Appiah had irresistibly shown his feeling written all over his body language that the king realised the unintended effect he had created from the coincidence of his use of words. Shortly after his arrival, Appiah had sincerely related his experience to the king.

'First, I wish to talk about the names your children bear. All of them, I have noticed, bear their native names including their Christian baptism names'

'Yes, your finding is not incorrect brother. It was actually deliberate. We realised early enough that names are important. Names bearing help a long way to foster vision of who we are and our people. European or Christian names, take it or leave it, foster for them the vision of their own people, vision of their own world and so our own names should foster the vision of our brothers too – not theirs. By the way, these people do not bear our own names. It is simply superiority complex on one hand and complex inferiority on the other hand. Please, I am talking to, and pleading with you, carry our African names wherever you go to foster vision of our brothers, vision of our fathers and vision of our own world.'

'Oh, this is profound. I also found out that your children read and study more African books and authors than the English and European'

'I will tell you something. When I entered the university to study, I met and learnt so much about arrogating and provoking impressions and pre-eminence of the Whiteman which suggested and supposed the reducibility of other cultures as margins, footnotes, pawns, slaves and less humans who were only created to serve loyally in his fields and plantations. The experience was not so bad because it alerted and woke something serious in me. It became a spiritual tonic and cure and mental liberation from the long-stayed abuse dehumanisation, cultural annihilation, inferiority complex, slavery and all categories of reducibility. It was a powerful release from the steady process of Europeanization/westernization, mental prostitution, cultural and human alienation, racial degradation. It was indeed a spiritual cure and jail break from the undue control, influences and subjugation of the white man to bravely and diligently embrace to start the serious journey of finding myself, discovering myself and being myself instead of any others. So, reading and studying African own authors, African books and African languages, like the names, is a sure way of fostering and installing vision of our own world, vision of our own image – not other over and above us as I encountered in the university.'

'I am indeed enjoying this conversation. You open my eyes. I should have also asked for other things like the general fashion sense. People here wear what they make than produced overseas. But I think you have the same explanation for it'

'Yes, eurocentricism is the mother of it all. Eurocentricism is the child of ethnocentricism. But the idea remains the same – putting one culture at the centre while the rest stay at the margin or cease from existing. Brother, we want our own existence, not to be shadow of others. So, we endeavour to use and sell our own products, our own fashion. Ours should compete too. We simply do not want to wait until when other cultures have totally dominated and submerged our existence. So, we emphasize much about our own. Don't forget it is our own people who make them, so it is fostering vision of our brothers and recognizing the gifts, talents and capacities we also have here not necessarily overseas. But ultimately, we are not talking of self-sufficiency. We are not self-sufficient and no one, no people are'

The king attended to few calls on the phone and, in the house, and the conversation went on. The servants ran errand within the premises. Other activities and discussions also took place in the house. His uncle, a lawyer and graduate from the University of Ibadan was inside his room quietly working and giving final touch to his briefs coming up the following day. The kingdom had given him as well as other team of legal practioneers in the kingdom many briefs pertaining the kingdom and other territories.

A certain woman of about thirty-five years old just arrived the king's house and would be talking with one of the king's aides on a contract. She was a professional fashion designer and had been contracted to produce the wears the kingdom would be using for the celebration of the king's coronation anniversary. The biggest book in the kingdom's library was the long voluminous encyclopaedia of the history of the kingdom written half a century ago by one of their own professional historians. Even the chief engineer, technicians, programmers and server manager of the information technology were around to meet with the king later in the day.

One thing was common about all these people. The king had fought tooth and nail with his own cabinet who opted to get most of these experts from outside and give the contracts to foreigners who were easily judged more competent and result-proven than the indigenes. But in the end, the king prevailed. All of them enjoyed the wise decision of the young king today for believing in and using their own people and they prayed for his long live. The king had vision of their own brothers. Not vision of aliens. The king stood up and walked around with his interlocutor. They discussed walking around the premises with beautiful and adorable look. Glass of water was brought for him by one of the maids and he carried a drink for the walk.

'You see brother, one thing you must not forget about is vision of your brothers; you must always strive to carry this with you, to see your brothers and sisters in your living. Yes, the whole world is our brother and sisters. We are educated to be universal citizens. I am a globalist myself. But don't forget that true charity starts at home. We must see and recognize our own brothers here first. You see many schools and learning institutions we have put in place. Some of our men and women have been missioned overseas to study, acquire knowledge and gather experiences. When they are done, and we have already started with the case of engineers Kofi, Nana and Majid, we will recall them home and put them in good strategic places and positions. We want our own doctors in our hospitals and surgical theatres; we want our own engineers and builders in building our factories, roads, bridges, towers, houses etc. We want our own scientists, technicians, experts and technocrats in all the relevant areas. We want our o own researchers, professors and scholars to build our own nation and build the world too by our contributions internationally and globally. We want our own writers, authors, publishers, educators and educationists. We want our own literatures and books. We want our own indigenous knowledge. And we want our children to be aware of this – no nation grows well without first growing within and looking inward, without growing itself or by depending practically on others. In fact, no individual does that let alone a people, a nation. We must fight core-periphery. We must fight dependence theory. We must stop dastard dependence. If we succeed, then we have fought decisively poverty and ignorance. If we succeed, then, we have fought diseases and all other ills and problems. If we succeed, we can turn around gladly and give ourselves resounding kudos, smile, laugh and shake hands and say we have done well. And we can say thank God. We can say we have found God. We can say proudly and gladly that we have known God. We cannot find or know God living on others, living for others. We want to do what David did. We want to build a people; we want to build a nation for him. Only then can we rejoice and be glad. We will not build for him foreign nations or foreign Gods but our own, our very own image, the vision of who we are – not others. Do you believe in all these Appiah my brother?'

'Oh yes, I do. I am truly overwhelmed. I understand your position. We can use our own capacities, potentials, powers, resources, talents, gifts, endowments to grow our economy, our faith, our finance, our science, our governance, our fashion, our literature, our learning and education. We can use African capacities to grow our industries and institutions. We can use African capacities to grow our people and our nation. I am with you my king, my brother'

'Then, you are welcomed. Let the good works begin'

'Appiah lied. He did not understand much of what he was saying. He was not with the king. He was leaving soon. His archenemy Stabo had not given up. But he did not know all this. Or he was quick to forget everything in a haste. Only another miracle will save him this time.

9

It was also perceived that Appiah's escape came from the

instruction received from God while in the dream in the prison. The promised blessings started to manifest in many ways. It started with Appiah being the first person to cross the stigmatized forest and return alive without any adverse consequence either on him or the kingdom. By doing this, he opened a big wide door of expansionism and developments in this town/kingdom. He released the people from their long term mental captivity in superstition. They, who feared before, now have the courage and readiness to go beyond their original land and to expand.

The stigmatized and demonized land happened to be the most fertile part of the kingdom. It was a great eye opener for the people. It was a new dawn for the kingdom. Appiah rescued a girl child of eight years old who was kidnapped days before his arrival to the kingdom. He was also gifted in poetry, painting, sculpture and interpretation of the laws. He studied agricultural science in school. He brought his knowledge to bear on the agriculture prosperity that highly uplifted the kingdom above all others.

This elevated him over above everyone in the king's palace, and many were jealous of him. In a short time, the best students started coming from this town as well as notable scientists, artists, inventors, financiers and notable citizens. The kingdom experienced tremendous growth and developments practically in all spheres of life but in a very short time which amazed so many people and challenged their counterparts and contemporaries and they grew envious and sad about the rapid progress of the city of Monotoso. They could not understand the promise of God coming to fulfilment through Appiah. In their envy, the other towns teamed up to bring the kingdom down. They found the chief persecutor very instrumental and a very strong partner in this mission. Discovering Appiah's place of exile, demands for his release under any cost and circumstances started.

The chief persecutor and others started to go to the kingdom again and again to seek or sometimes, protest for Appiah's release making all their false allegations as usual. As they went, the king kept turning them down and saying no to their demands. Stabo and his team approached the king countless number of times more than Moses approached pharaoh for the release of Israelites. In the Monotoso kingdom, it was the long demand for the release of Appiah.

After sometime, what started in a state of non-violence, dialogue and astute diplomacy graduated and gravitated to heightened tensions, threats, fears and wars. All other cities teamed up in a strong alliance to pull down the kingdom and all its glamour. It was equally somewhat a battle for supremacy.

It was then that the king started consulting with his cabinet again and again. In one of the deliberations, they decided to check the Holy Bible thoroughly which again was a big gift and blessing Appiah propagated to the kingdom – the message or good news of Christ. They searched, searched, searched, searched, searched, searched…and searched. They searched the scripture morning to night and sometimes morning to morning. They did not sleep. They did not rest. Finally, they came upon the injunction,

Instead of the whole nation to die, it is better for one man to die.

The decision was so difficult for the king to make but his hands were tied, and he could not do otherwise. Just few days after the release of Appiah to the chief persecutor and he was killed, serious calamity and chaos befall the kingdom. People became to die in strange ways. Other strange things began to happen. Today, it was one story. Tomorrow, it was another story. No one was sure what would happen next. All the blessings and glories that come with Appiah seemed to have suddenly disappeared with his exit and gruesome murder.

At this time they also consulted among themselves. The king consulted with his men again and again, and finally they sought the great counsel of the preacher. The preacher, it was, who said to them boldly and truthfully that the cause for the catastrophe was the innocent man that was released to his persecutors. They were shocked hearing this. They stood in awe and speechless. Every part of them went damn weak. Their kneels knocked. Their both hands trembled, their stomach chuckled. They knew nothing to do or say. Or they knew. They challenged back and boldly,

But we acted upon the sacred injunction of the scripture. We searched thoroughly through the scripture. We were guided spiritually by the Bible. We looked into the Bible.

At that very point, the interjection of the preacher cooed,

You should have looked into his eyes to find the truth

'Are you serious about this, preacher? Are you kidding me? Could we not have honoured the law, the biblical injunction at that? What is this new way you have brought to our land?'

'You heard me right. That is exactly where you went wrong. There is always a big trouble doing what you did; you should not have only looked into the scripture but ultimately, you should have looked into the man's eyes. You should have looked into your brother's eyes for many truths are written and concealed in our human faces than found in the books or scripture. You should have looked deeper into his eyes. The terrifying trouble with the world is that we are given to preaching heavenly eye without earthly eye; we get indulged in seeing visions of saints and angels without noticing the next brother or sister'.

The king's head was down for a long time. Inwardly, he realized it was no new way, it was no new teaching. Brotherhood was what he preached. He preached brotherhood and defended more than royalty. Yet, here he was so helpless, weak and empty in what his energy flowed for. Now he realized so painfully that the strongest fighter of a course can equally assumed the weakest.